CLINTON TOWNSHIP PUBLIC LIB

3854200010914

P9-DNY-902

J Merrill, Bob
+
Me   How Much Is that Doggie
            in The Window? 22296
CLINTON TOWNSHIP
Public Library
Waterman, Illinois

DEMCO

How Much Is That Doggie in the Window?

Whispering Coyote Press

BOSTON

How Much Is That Doggie in the Window?

With best wishes!

[signature]

Words and Music by **Bob Merrill**

As retold and illustrated by

IZA TRAPANI

Published by Whispering Coyote Press
300 Crescent Court, Suite 860
Dallas, TX 75201
"(How Much Is) That Doggie In The Window," words and music by Bob Merrill, copyright © 1953,
renewed 1981, Golden Bell Songs.
Adaptation and illustrations copyright © 1997 by Iza Trapani

All rights reserved including the right of reproduction in whole or in part in any form.
Printed in Hong Kong
10 9 8 7 6 5 4 3 2

Book design and production by *The Kids at Our House*
Text set in 22-point Goudy Old Style Bold

Library of Congress Cataloging-in-Publication Data
Trapani, Iza
How much is that doggie in the window? / by Iza Trapani; adapted from original musical score
by Bob Merrill.
p.   cm.
Summary: Longing to buy a special puppy, a boy tries to find the money he needs but ends up spending it
on family members, who ultimately surprise him with the dog as a gift.
ISBN 1–879085–74–7
1. Children's songs—Texts.   [1. Dogs—Songs and music.   2. Money—Songs and music.   3. Songs.]
I. Merrill, Bob.   How much is that doggie in the window?   II. Title.
PZ8.3.T686Ho   1997
782.42164´0268—dc20
[E]   96–42004
                                                                                      CIP
                                                                                       AC

That doggie's on sale for sixty dollars.
I'd even take five dollars off.
But you only have eleven fifty
I'm sorry, but that's not enough.

Perhaps you would rather buy a hamster,
A gerbil or maybe some mice?
These lizards and snakes are simply splendid.
I'll take fifty cents off the price.

Oh no mister, no, I want that doggie
Just look how he's wagging at me.
I'll go find a way to make some money
And I'll buy him, just wait and see.

Clinton Township Public Library
Waterman, Illinois

I thought I'd sell lemonade on Monday—
Now that's a good plan, don't you think?
But it rained all day and most of Tuesday
And no one came out for a drink.

On Wednesday and Thursday I felt lousy—
I had a bad cold in my head.
The weather was great, but I was achy
And had to spend two days in bed.

On Friday my little baby sister
Fell down and she banged up her knee.
I went out and bought her frozen yogurt
And she was as pleased as could be.

On Saturday Mom was in the garden—
A bee stung her right on the toe.
I went out and bought her chocolate candy.
It made her feel better, you know.

On Sunday my Daddy got allergic.
He sneezed and his eyes itched real bad.
I went out and bought a box of tissues
And spent almost all that I had.

So that's why I didn't earn a penny.
I guess that I'm plain out of luck.
Last Monday I had eleven fifty
And now I have less than a buck.

Oh, where is that doggie in the window?
Oh, where did that cute doggie go?
I know that I can't afford to buy him.
I just thought I'd come say, "Hello."

Some people stopped in and bought that doggie
For their very special young son.
They bought him the dog so they could thank him
For all the nice things he had done.

Can that be the doggie from the window?
I wonder can that really be?
Oh, what a surprise! I never figured
That lucky young boy would be me.

Clinton Township Public Library
Waterman, Illinois

How Much is that Doggie in the Window?

How much is that dog - gie in the win - dow? The one with the wag - gel - y tail. How much is that dog - gie in the win - dow? I do hope that dog - gie's for sale.

2. That doggie's on sale for sixty dollars.
   I'd even take five dollars off.
   But you only have eleven fifty
   I'm sorry, but that's not enough.

3. Perhaps you would rather buy a hamster,
   A gerbil or maybe some mice?
   These lizards and snakes are simply splendid.
   I'll take fifty cents off the price.

4. Oh no mister, no, I want that doggie
   Just look how he's wagging at me.
   I'll go find a way to make some money
   And I'll buy him, just wait and see.

5. I thought I'd sell lemonade on Monday—
   Now that's a good plan, don't you think?
   But it rained all day and most of Tuesday
   And no one came out for a drink.

6. On Wednesday and Thursday I felt lousy—
   I had a bad cold in my head.
   The weather was great, but I was achy
   And had to spend two days in bed.

7. On Friday my little baby sister
   Fell down and she banged up her knee.
   I went out and bought her frozen yogurt
   And she was as pleased as could be.

8. On Saturday Mom was in the garden—
   A bee stung her right on the toe.
   I went out and bought her chocolate candy.
   It made her feel better, you know.

9. On Sunday my Daddy got allergic.
   He sneezed and his eyes itched real bad.
   I went out and bought a box of tissues
   And spent almost all that I had.

10. So that's why I didn't earn a penny.
    I guess that I'm plain out of luck.
    Last Monday I had eleven fifty
    And now I have less than a buck.

11. Oh, where is that doggie in the window?
    Oh, where did that cute doggie go?
    I know that I can't afford to buy him.
    I just thought I'd come say, "Hello."

12. Some people stopped in and bought that doggie
    For their very special young son.
    They bought him the dog so they could thank him
    For all the nice things he had done.

13. Can that be the doggie from the window?
    I wonder can that really be?
    Oh, what a surprise! I never figured
    That lucky young boy would be me.